Gustavo Adolfo Bécquer, Mason Carnes

**Poems of Gustavo Adolfo Bécquer**

Gustavo Adolfo Bécquer, Mason Carnes

**Poems of Gustavo Adolfo Bécquer**

ISBN/EAN: 9783337407407

Printed in Europe, USA, Canada, Australia, Japan

Cover: Foto ©Andreas Hilbeck / pixelio.de

More available books at **www.hansebooks.com**

# POEMS

OF

## GUSTAVO ADOLFO BECQUER.

RENDERED INTO ENGLISH VERSE BY

## MASON CARNES.

TO

# MANUEL DE SANTA MARIA.

THE soft strings of a Spanish lute one day
　　You struck, and plaintive notes gushed forth
　　　　like tears.
Ravished I listened, and I longed to play
　　The music to another people's ears.

You showed me all the cunning workmanship,
　　The stretching of the strings, the exquisite
Adjustment of the frets, the body's dip ;
　　I took the lute and tried to copy it.

Well, here it is, re-fashioned and re-strung.
　　Play on it; ah, I fear those sweet, sad airs
Sound cracked and harsh now, better left unsung.
　　Well, fling the lute aside and take Becquer's !

TO

# GUSTAVO ADOLFO BECQUER.

*(Born 17th February, 1836.   Died 22nd December, 1870.)*

FULL twenty years since thy soul ceased to fight
　With tyrant matter and his thousand slaves,
　Opened Death's gate, plunged in the lake which
　　laves
The soul, dew-dripping rose and winged its flight
　　　Into eternal light.

Poor weary soul, hast thou at length release ?
　Doth the hag Sorrow curse with lusty Pain,
　And beat against the gate of Death in vain ?
Art thou immersed in joys that never cease,
　　　In never-ending peace ?

Art thou a note in that great hymn which thou
　Didst hear ? a line of beauty and the feel,
　The perfume of a rose ?   To love so leal,
Dost know its full perfection, what and how
　　　'Tis in the Ever-Now ?

Oh, if there be a better to each best,
　If thou dost soar in endless cycles of
　Large motion, upward soar !   If not, with love,
With perfect love and peace and beauty blest,
　　　Sweet soul, for ever rest !

M. C.

*22nd December,* 1890.

# INTRODUCTION.

GUSTAVO ADOLFO BECQUER, the son of a celebrated painter of Seville, was born in that city the 17th of February, 1836. Early left an orphan, he was educated under the care of his godmother at the school of San Antonio Abad, and afterwards at the naval school of San Telmo, where he remained but a short time. His godmother then determined to make a merchant of him, and directed his studies accordingly; but reading books was much more to his taste than keeping books, and he turned his uninteresting ledgers into sketch-books with much skill and humour. Encouraged by the success of his early verses, he determined to enter the arena of literature, and fight there for fame and fortune with an independence and strength of will astonishing in one so frail in health, so sweet and amiable in temperament. So, in 1854, against the wishes of his guardian, and sacrificing the prospects of the fortune she intended to leave him, he boldly set out for Madrid, with many hopes and little else.

Like many another similar capitalist, he soon found

himself bankrupt, for his hopes dwindled away day by day as he saw his pen bringing him little more than bread and water, and that not regularly. So, finally, with his friend and future biographer and editor, Ramon Rodriguez Correa, he accepted a small post in the Department of Public Works. Always of delicate health, endowed with a dreamy artistic temperament, and totally unfitted for the monotonous, deadening routine of a clerk's life, he proved a poor public servant, and was politely dismissed with a small pension.

Attacked by a terrible malady, with poverty in his home and death at his door, he struggled bravely on, writing for *El Contemporáneo* his most famous prose work, " Cartas desde mi celda," numberless stories, learned essays on architecture, of which he was passionately fond, translations, and even political and critical articles, in which the correctness of his taste and the excellence of his judgment were often nullified by the goodness of his heart.

In 1862 his brother Valeriano, having made some success as a painter in Seville, came to Madrid to live with him. They joined their forces against misfortunes and disappointments, and fought with courage, with even hope. While making ill-paid sketches, Valeriano dreamed of being able some day to buy canvases on which to paint his large conceptions ; and Gustavo, toiling over the translation of an insipid novel, would long for time to give form to the magnificent ideas with which his fertile brain teemed, and which he feared—alas! too truly— would descend into the grave with him, unuttered and lost for ever.

A day of respite and of joy came at last, but death followed quickly in its wake, for in September, 1870, Valeriano died. From this shock poor Gustavo never recovered, and on the 22nd of the following December he breathed his last sigh.

After his death his prose works and his "Rimas," with an introduction by Correa, were published by subscription for the benefit of widows and orphans; and these two volumes are all that were left by the fecund brain that had conceived and planned in detail a marvellously long list of plays, stories, essays, and poems.

Patient and uncomplaining with his friends, he unburdened himself in poetry, pouring forth all his sorrows and longings in his "Rimas," which alone have gained for him an undying fame in his own country. For the sadness, beauty, passion, and originality of these lyrics, Becquer has been compared frequently with Heine and de Musset; and Correa especially calls attention to the likeness of the "Rimas" to the "Intermezzo" of Heine, inasmuch as each may be regarded as one poem, embodying the joys (few enough with poor Becquer), the sufferings, the aspirations, and the life of a poet.

M. C.

# POEMS.

# POEMS.

———◆———

THROUGH all my being rolls a hymn deep-toned
  And wild, presaging in my spirit's night
A dawn.   These pages are its cadences
  That through the sombre shadows wing their flight.


Would I could tame man's poor rebellious tongue,
  Enriching it with meaning newly-found,
And write with words of passion that would be
  At once both sighs and smiles, colour and sound !


But 'tis in vain.   There is no frame to hold
  And to express such music.   Should I, dear,
Feel e'en thy soft hand's touch, I could not speak ;
  My kissed lips could not tell thee what I hear !

## II.

FLYING arrow that darts astray,
　Shot at misfortune unforeseen,
　Without divining where its keen
Quivering edge will find its way;

Leaf that from the sapless tree
　Is ravished by the wild south wind,
　With none to know or care to find
The furrow where its end will be;

Gigantic wave,—which the tempest hurls
　And fiercely tosses upon the sea—
　That rolling and raging wantonly
Knows not the shore towards which it whirls;

Light that shines though death be nigh
　And burns in flickering circles small,
　Not knowing which among them all
Will flicker the last and trembling die;

Such am I.  By chance I flow
　Into this troubled world unsought;
　I ebb away without a thought
Of whence I come or where I go.

### III.

STRANGE shock that thrills our being
And through our thoughts runs riot,
Like a fierce tempest raging
    That puts the waves to rout ;

Murmur that through the spirit
Rises and goes increasing,
Like a volcano rumbling,
    Foretelling flame and death ;

Images vague and misty
Of weird and monstrous beings ;
Vistas that vanish swiftly
    As if across a veil ;

Harmonious, blending colours,
That on the air are limning
The atoms of the rainbow
    Which stray in strands of light.

Thoughts without words, expression,
And words without a meaning ;
Wild cadences that wander,
    Rhythmless and measureless.

Longings to weep and sudden
Flashes of joy ; strange wishes,
Memories dim and misty
  Of things that never were ;

Nervous energy vainly
Striving to find an outlet ;
A wingèd steed swift-speeding
  Through space, unbridled, wild ;

Madness that thrills and kindles
And raises high the spirit ;
Of genius creative
  Ebriety divine——
    Such is Inspiration.

Gigantic voice that orders
The brain's anarchic chaos
And hurls swift through the shadows
  A thunderbolt of light ;

Strong dazzling golden bridle
That curbs the flying courser—
The mind, wild and ecstatic—
  And checks its mad career ;

Sun, through the dark clouds bursting
And reaching proud the zenith ;
Strong thread of light in fagots
      For ever binding thoughts ;


Skilled hand, for ever trying
To string rich words together
(Like pearls upon a necklace)
      Upon the strands of thought ;


Harmonious rhythm, ensnaring
With cadence and with number,
Caging within the measure
      The fluttering bird-like notes ;


Chisel that cuts the marble,
Seeking the hidden statue,
And to the form ideal
      Fashions the massive block ;


Strange air in which revolving
Thoughts go in rhythmic order,
Like atoms round some magnet
      Whirling in circles swift ;

Torrent whose water quenches
The thirst of burning fever ;
Oasis, to the spirit
  Restoring all its strength ;—
    Such is reason !

 With both in strife for ever,
Of both for ever master,
Thus, only thus, can genius
  For ever yoke the two.

## IV.

AH ! do not say that, all its treasure spent,
For lack of subjects mute the lyre has grown :
Perchance no poets there will be, but still
       For ever poetry will live.

While the waves enkindled by the kiss of light all
    palpitate,
While the sun adorns the broken clouds with robes of
    fire and gold ;
While the air bears harmonies and perfumes in its ample
    lap,
While there is a spring to glad the world, there will be
    poetry !

While Science strives in vain to find the origin of life,
And in the sea or sky remains unsounded one abyss ;
While mankind advancing ever knows not whither trend
    his steps,
While there is a mystery for man, there will be poetry !

While we feel the soul rejoicing with no laughter from
    the lips ;
While we feel the soul lamenting with no tears to cloud
    the eye ;

While the fiery heart continues battling with the sober
　　head,
While there are remembrances and hopes, there will be
　　poetry !


While there are some eyes reflecting other eyes that look
　　at them,
While a sighing lip remains responsive to a lip that
　　sighs,
While two blended, mingled souls can feel each other in
　　a kiss,
While one beauteous woman still remains, there will be
　　poetry !

## V.

SPIRIT without a name,
Essence ineffable,
I live with life without
A form that mind can shape.

I swim in space, trembling
Before the sun's hot blaze,
'Mid shadows palpitate
And float away with mists.

I am the fringe of gold
Of the far-distant star ;
I am the light serene
And cold of the high mocn.

I am the burning cloud
That trembles in the west ;
I am the luminous wake
Of planets wandering.

I'm snow upon the heights
And fire upon the sands,
Blue wave upon the seas
And foam upon the strands.

A note in the sweet lute,
A perfume in the rose,
Will-o'-the-wisp in tombs,
Ivy on ruins old.


I thunder in the stream,
I crackle in the flame,
I blind in lightning and
I shriek and roar in storms.


I laugh upon the hills,
I murmur on the plant,
I sigh upon the wave
And weep on the dry leaf.


Slowly I undulate
With atoms of the smoke
That rises gently to
The sky in spirals large.


Upon the golden threads
The insects hang in air
I swing and swing between
The trees at hottest noon—

I chase the wanton nymphs
Who, in the current of
The sylvan rivulet,
Naked sport playfully ;


And in the coral-wood,
Rich carpeted with pearls,
I follow in the sea
The Naiads swift of foot.


In hollow grottoes where
The sun ne'er penetrates,
Mingling with all the gnomes,
I gaze upon their wealth.


I seek the tracks effaced
Of centuries gone by,
I know of kingdoms which
Have left not e'en a name.


I follow giddily
The worlds as they revolve
My eye embraces all
The universe at once.

I know of regions where
No murmur ever comes,
And where unshapen stars
Hope for a breath of life.

I am the bridge that spans
The dread abyss ; I am
The unknown ladder that
Unites the sky to earth.

I am the wondrous ring
Invisible that binds
The world of matter to
The larger world of mind.

I am that spirit free,
Essence unknowable,
Perfume unknown, of which
The poet is the vase !

### VI.

OE'R the field of battle in bloody dress,
　　In the silence drear of the sombre night,
Passes the breeze, in a sweet caress
　　　Perfumes and harmonies bringing.

So, symbol of sorrow and tenderness,
　　In her heart a chill, on her mind a blight,
Passes Ophelia in dire distress,
　　　Plucking wild flowers and singing.

### VII.

IN the dark corner of the drawing-room,
　　Forgotten by its mistress long ago,
Silent, cover'd with dust there in the gloom
　　　The old harp lies.

How many notes slept in those strings half-dead
　　And waited for her fingers, white as snow,
To wake them into throbbing life, that fled
　　　Away in sighs !

Ah me ! thought I, how oft sleeps genius thus
　　Deep in the soul, hoping eternally
A voice will say, as He to Lazarus,
　　　" Arise and walk."—Ah me !

### VIII.

WHEN I see the blue horizon in the distance melt away
Through a veil of dust that blazes with the burning heat
    of day,
It seems possible to snatch me from all earthly, wretched
    things
And to soar, dissolved in atoms, on those golden, misty
    wings.

When I see the stars at midnight in the dark depths of
    the skies
Trembling, shimmering with passion like a million ardent
    eyes,
It seems possible to seek them, where they shine, in rapid
    flight,
And to merge me in their being in a burning kiss of
    light.

Deep in doubt my faith is sunken, but these longings are
    a sign
That I bear within me something that's immortal and
    divine !

## IX.

BALMY breezes softly sighing,
　　Kiss the light waves as they curl ;
And the sun, albeit dying
　　Kisses warm yon cloud of pearl ;
For a kiss the flame is trying
　　Round the burning log to whirl ;
And the willow never misses
Giving back the river's kisses !

## X.

THE air-beams invisible wings unfold
　　And restlessly glowing soar over the earth,
The heavens melt into rays of gold,
　　While the earth is trembling with nervous mirth.

I close my eyes and I hear, spell-bound,
　　A cadence of kisses, a beating of wings
In billows of harmony floating around ;—
　　'Tis Love that passes, while Nature sings !

XI.

" I AM the symbol of passion,
      Ardent and dark, with a soul
    That is full of desire for enjoyment.
      Seekest thou me? "—" Not thee."

" Pale, golden-locked, I can give thee
      Exquisite joy without end ;
    There's a treasure of tenderness in me—
      Callest thou me ? "—" Not thee."

" I am a dream, an impossible something,
      A phantom of mist and light ;
    Intangible, bodyless, love thee
      I cannot."   " O come thou, come ! "

## XII.

BECAUSE your eyes are green, child, like the deep
You fain would weep :
The Naiad's eyes were greenish-blue,
Minerva's too,
Green are the houris' eyes
In Paradise.

Green is the gay adornment of the woodland in the
spring,
Amid the seven colours of the rainbow mark its sheen,
The emerald, the badge of hope to which the faithful
cling,
The mighty waves, the laurel of the poet—all are green.

Within your cheek a rosebud curls
Itself, then blushes through the pearls.
And yet you grieve,
For you believe
Your eyes disfigure it. Ah ! no,
It is not so.
Restless and green your eyes
Like almond leaves appear,
That thrill at the air's sighs
In loving fear.

Your mouth is a pomegranate burst,
Inviting one to quench one's thirst.
  And yet you grieve,
  For you believe
Your eyes disfigure it.   Ah ! no,
  It is not so.
  Your eyes gleaming with ire,
  Mad waves appear to be,
That on the rocks expire
  Fearless and free.

## XIII.

YOUR eye is blue ; when you're laughing,
  Its soft mellow light brings to me
The tremulous sheen of the morning
  That glitters upon the sea.

Your eye is blue ; when you're weeping,
  The mischievous tears I espy
Look like dew-drops that shimmer and sparkle
  On a violet modestly shy.

Your eye is blue ; and when from it
  Dart forth in their mad career
Your thoughts, in the sky of the even
  Like falling stars they appear.

### XIV.

I SAW you but an instant, yet your eyes
Image themselves before mine own and rise
And float, like that dark spot, mantled in blaze
Which floats and blinds, when on the sun you gaze.

Wherever I may look, I do but turn
To see your glowing eyes that flash and burn ;
But 'tis not you that I encounter, for
It is your look alone, your eyes—no more !

I see them in the corner of my room
Wildly and strangely shining in the gloom ;
And even when I sleep I feel them there
Wide-open, fix'd on me with steady stare.

I know that there are will-o'-the-wisps that fly
Before the traveller, leading him to die ;
Your eyes draw me along ; I feel 'tis so,
But yet I know not whither they would go.

### XV.

FLOATING veil of misty light,
Ribbon curl'd of foam snow-white,
Cadence bold from harp of gold,
Wave of light and kiss of breeze,—
    Such are you !

You, an airy shade that flees
When I try its form to seize ;
Vanishing like flame o'erthrown,
Like the fog and murmured moan
    From a lake of blue.

Wave on shoreless sea, a trace
Of a meteor through space,
Long desire for something higher,
Deep lamenting of the wind,
    Such am I !

I, who in my pain will find
Toward your own my eyes inclined,
I, who mad and tireless run
After shadows of the sun,
    Visions floating by !

### XVI.

IF, when the bell-flow'rs on your balcony
    All trembling lie,
You think it is the sighing, murmuring wind
    That passes by,
Know that, hidden among the green leaves there,
    For you I sigh.

If, when behind you echoing on your ear
    Vague murmurs fall,
You think some far-off voice has called you, know
    That from the pall
Of evening shadows that surround you, love,
    To you I call.

If in the dead of night your timorous heart
    Beats fast, while near
Your lips you feel a passionate, burning breath,
    Ah! have no fear.
Know that, although invisible, I breathe
    Beside you, dear.

### XVII.

To-DAY there's a smile on the earth and the skies,
  To-day to my soul comes the sun's brightest ray,
To-day I have seen her, I've basked in her eyes,—
    In God I believe to-day!


### XVIII.

TIRED by the ball and out of breath,
  Her cheeks warm with the roses' bloom,
Leaning upon my arm she stopped
    At one end of the room—

Beneath the palpitating gauze,
  Moved at the bidding of her breast,
A flow'r trembled in movement sweet
    And measured—rhythmic rest!

As in a nacre cradle there,
  Toward which the wanton zephyr trips,
Perchance it slept, kiss'd by the breath
    Of those half-open lips.

Thought I : Ah! who could let Time slip
  Away so coldly, carelessly?
And oh, if flowers sleep, how sweet,
    How sweet its dream must be!

XIX.

WHEN you lean on your bosom your head
  O'ershadowed with gloom,
Like a beauteous lily you seem,
  Plucked in its bloom.


On giving you purity, love,
  In the self-same mould,
God fashioned the lily and you
  Of snow and gold !


XX.

IF sometimes you feel that an atmosphere burning
  Enkindles your lips as by chance,
Know that the eyes that can utter their yearning
  Can also kiss with a glance !

### XXI.

WHAT is poetry? (I bask
  In the sheen of eyes of blue)
What is poetry, you ask?
  Poetry?—'tis you!

### XXII.

NE'ER until now have I seen anywhere
  A flower that on a volcano grows,
But next to your heart I see nestling a rose;—
  Tell me, how lives it there?

### XXIII.

FOR a look, the world I would give,
  For a smile, all of Heaven's bliss,
For a kiss—ah! I do not know
  What I'd give you, dear, for a kiss!

### XXIV.

Two blood-red tongues of fire
That, circling the same log,
Approach and as they kiss
Form but a single flame;

Two notes, plucked cunningly
Together·from the lute,
That meet in space in sweet
Harmonious embrace;

Two waves that come to die
Together on the beach
And, as they're breaking, crown
Themselves with silver crest;

Two sinuous curls of smoke
That rise from out the lake
And, as they meet there in
The sky, form one white cloud;

Two thoughts that equally
Gush out; two kisses blent;
Two echoes mingling e'er,—
Like these are our two souls!

## XXV.

WHEN sleep folds his gauzy wings
Over you at dead of night,
And your eye-lashes fast-closed
Look like bows of ebony ;
Then to listen to your heart
Throbbing in a sweet unrest
And to lean your sleeping head
On my breast, I'd give, my soul,
All I own—light, air and thought !

When your eyes look far away
At some thing invisible,
And the reflex of a smile
Darts, illumining your lips ;
Then to read upon your brow
Silent thoughts, that pass like clouds
O'er a glass, I'd give, my soul,
All I wish—fame, genius, gold !

When words die upon your lips,
And your breath comes quick and warm,
And your cheeks are all aglow
And your black eyes look in mine ;

Then to see in them a spark,
Flashing with a humid fire,
As it gushes from the heart,
I would give, soul of my soul,
All that is and all to come !

### XXVI.

Awake, I fear to look ;
Asleep, I dare to see ;
For that, soul of my soul,
I watch the while you sleep.

Awake, you laugh ; and laughing your unquiet lips appear
Like sinuous, crimson meteors upon a sky of snow.
Asleep, a sweet smile gently curls the corners of your
mouth,
Soft as the track effulgent of the swiftly dying sun ;—
Sleep ! Sleep !

Awake, you look ; and looking your moist eyes resplendent
shine
Like a wave, whose crest is smitten by a jav'lin of the sun.
Asleep, across your eye-lids you send forth a tranquil
sheen,
Like a lamp transparent, shedding even rays of tempered
light ;—
Sleep ! Sleep !

Awake, you speak ; and speaking, all your vibrant words
appear
Like a show'r of pearls in torrents pour'd into a golden
cup.

Asleep, in ev'ry murmur of your soft and measured
    breath
I listen to a poem, which my soul enamour'd hears;—
         Sleep!  Sleep!

    On my heart I've placed my hand
    Lest its beating should be heard,
    Lest discordant it should sound
    On the solemn chord of night.

    I have closed the jalousies
    Lest that roysterer, the dawn,
    With his glaring robe of light
    Should awake you from your dreams;
       Sleep!  Sleep!

### XXVII.

    WHEN within the shadows drear
    Murmuring a voice complains,
    Breaks the silence with sad strains,
    If within my heart I hear

Sweetly sounding every note;
Tell me, is't the wind that dies
So lamenting, or your sighs
Speaking love-words as they float?

When at morn the sunbeams steal
Through my window, and I trace
On their shifting sheen your face,
If the touch I think I feel
Of two other lips; am I,
Tell me, merely mad, distraught,
Or with melting kisses fraught
Does your heart send out a sigh?

If within my soul be found
Naught but you from dazzling light,
Naught but you from gloomy night,
Naught but you from all around
Deep-reflected ev'rywhere;
Tell me, do I feel and think
In a dream, or do I drink
Ev'ry sigh you breathe like air?

### XXVIII.

Upon her lap she held an open book ;
Her soft black tresses kiss'd my cheek ; no look
Cast we upon the words, nor looked we round
But both maintain'd a silence most profound.
E'en then I could not tell how long 'twas kept ;
I only know that naught was heard except
The quicken'd breath, which from our warm lips crept ;
I only know we two together turned,
Our eyes met, in a kiss our blent lips burned.

Dante's " Inferno " was the book.   My head
Bent o'er it.   " Do you understand," I said,
" How in one line may be a poem ? "   And
She answered, blushing ; " Yes, I understand."

### XXIX.

A tear rose to her eyes, and to my lips
   The word of pardon she desired ;
   Pride spoke, her weeping ceased, the word
      Upon my lips expired.          .
I go by one road, by another she ;
   But thinking on our mutual lot
   I ask, why was I silent then ?
      And she, why wept I not ?

### XXX.

Our love was a tragic farce
　　In which the grave and the gay
Were so blent that a tear and a smile
　　O'er the face together would stray.

But the worst of the play was this,
　　That when the curtain fell,
We both had the tears, 'tis true,
　　But she kept the smiles as well !

### XXXI.

She passed triumphant in her beauty, and
　　　　I let her pass ;
To even look at her I turned not round,
Yet something murmured in my ear, " 'Tis she."

Who joined the ev'ning to the morning?　That
　　　　I know not, but
I know that one short summer night the dawn
Was wedded to the twilight, and—" it was."

XXXII.

'Tis nothing—merely a question of words·—
   And yet neither you nor I
Will ever agree, after what has passed,
   On whom the blame should lie.

A dictionary of love !—What a shame
   There is none !  We might look inside
And see when pride is dignity,
   And when it is simply pride !

### XXXIII.

SHE passes mute ; her movements light and free
         Are silent harmony ;
Her steps recall, heard in the twilight dim,
The rhythmic cadence of a wingèd hymn.

She looks with eyes half-open, with those eyes
         As bright as Paradise ;
And all the planets in celestial flight,
Seeking those limpid deeps, glow with new light.

She laughs, — the echoes of a woodland stream
         The merry ripples seem ;
She weeps, and ev'ry tear's a soft caress,
A poem of unbounded tenderness.

Perfume and light exhaling, lustrous, warm
         In colour, and in form
Voluptuous, expression too has she—
That everlasting fount of poesy.

Stupid?   Bah !   If the secret never slips
         From out her pretty lips,
What any other says is dull as lead
To what she leaves so charmingly unsaid !

### XXXIV.

THE occasional tenderness you display
   Surprises me more than your cold neglect,
For what little good may be in my clay
   You could never suspect !

### XXXV.

IF, in a book, of all our wrongs
   The story should be traced,
And in our souls, as on its leaves,
   They should be all effaced,
I love you so, your love has left
   Such traces in my breast,
That were you to blot out one wrong,
   I'd blot out all the rest !

### XXXVI.

BEFORE you I shall die; for in my heart
   The dagger may be found
With which your small hand open'd ruthlessly
   The broad and mortal wound.

Before you I shall die; my spirit, firm
   And constant in its love,
Patiently sitting at the gate of Death
   Will wait for you above.

The days fly with the hours and with the days
   The years too swiftly pass,
And you will call at length at that dread gate,—
   Who fails to call, alas?

Then, as the quiet earth guards silently
   Your sin and your remains,
When in the waves of death you plunge your soul
   To wash away its stains;

There, where life's murmur trembling goes to die,
   Like flames of fading fire,
Like waves that gently ripple to the shore
   And silently expire;

D

There, where the sepulchre shuts out the night
   And shows eternal day,—
There we must speak ; then all we've kept unsaid
   We two will have to say.


### XXXVII.

A SIGH is but air, and melts into air,
A tear is but water and to the sea flows.
Tell me, woman, when love is forgot,
      Do you know where it goes ?


### XXXVIII.

WHY tell me that ?   I know it ; she is vain,
Haughty, capricious, fickle as the wind ;
Water would gush out from a sterile rock
Sooner than any feeling from her soul.

I know that in her heart—a serpent's nest—
There's not a fibre that would thrill to love,
That she is but a soulless statue—yet
      She is so beautiful !

## XXXIX.

You were the storm and I the lofty tow'r
  That dared defy your pow'r ;
You had to dash yourself against my wall
  Or hurl me to my fall,—
        It could not be !

You were the ocean, I the firm, grim rock
  That e'er withstood your shock ;
You had to root me up or roll and roar
  And break upon the shore,—
        It could not be !

You, beautiful, were wont to win the field,
  I, proud, to never yield ;
Narrow the path, the shock none could endure
  Inevitably sure,—
        It could not be !


## XL.

When they related it I felt as if
An icy blade of steel had pierced me through ;
I leaned against the wall, and, for a time
Benumbed, lost consciousness of where I was.

Night fell upon my spirit, and my soul
In anger and in pity was submerged,—
And then I understood how one could weep,
And then I understood how one could kill !

The heavy cloud of sorrow rolled away ;
With pain I stammered out a few short words.
Who told the news ?   A faithful friend.   It was
An honest, worthy deed,—I gave him thanks.


### XLI.

I PUT the light aside, and sat me down
Upon the edge of the disorder'd bed ;
At the blank wall I gazed, immovable,
        Mute, sombre, like the dead.

And how long was I there ?   I do not know ;
When grief's dull drunkenness was leaving me,
The light was out and on my balconies
        The sun laughed gleefully.

Nor do I know in those dread hours of what
I thought or what mad passions through me roll'd ;
But I remember that I wept and curst,
And that, ere morning came, I had grown old.

### XLII.

As in an open book
  I read in the depths of your eyes ;
What good to feign with the lip
  A smile which the eye denies ?

Weep ! that you've loved me awhile
  Do not blush to confess with a tear.
Weep ! no one's looking,—you see
  I'm a man, yet I'm weeping, dear !


### XLIII.

Upon the keystone of a tottering arch,—
Tinged red by time,—the work of chisels old
And rude, a Gothic blazon showed itself,
        Crested and bold.

The ivy, that was clinging thick behind
The granite plumes which from the helmet start,
Obscured the scutcheon, whereon was a hand
        Holding a heart.

To look at this in the deserted square
        Together stood we two :
She said, " This is the faithful emblem of
        My love—constant and true."

Ay, what she told me then is truth itself—
      Truth that she'll ever go,
Her heart upon her hand or anywhere
      Save in her breast,—there, no !

### XLIV.

SHE, hiding in the shadows, wounded me,
Sealing her treason with a kiss.  Her part
She knew too well ; around my neck her arms
  She threw, then stabbed me through the heart.
How can she boldly laugh and gaily sing
And still pursue her path, with roses rife ?
Because no blood flows from the wound, because
  Death sometimes wears the robes of Life !

### XLV.

OVER the deep abysses of the earth
  I've looked, and of the sky,
And I have seen them to the end in thought
  Or with the eye.
But oh, I came across a heart's abyss
  And leaned far over ; back
My soul and eyes fell in dismay—it was
  So deep, so black !

### XLVI.

As one draws from a wound the sword,
   From out my heart my love I drew,
Although I felt, on doing it,
   That with it life was wrested too.

Her image, shrined within my soul,
   From the high altar down I wrenched,
The light of faith that on it burned
   Before the empty shrine was quenched—

Yet still to struggle with my will
   Her face with everything comes blended,—
How can I with that dream e'er sleep—
   That dream in which all dreaming ended

### XLVII.

Sometimes I meet her passing by;
     A smile I see
Upon her lips.   How can she laugh?
     I ask.

Another smile comes to my lips—
     Dull sorrow's mask—
And then I think ;—perchance she laughs
     Like me !

### XLVIII.

ACCORDING to his fancy from a log
The savage fashions for himself a god,
And then bows down before his own rude work
And humbly worships,—so did you and I.

Reality we gave to what was but
A phantom—mere illusion of the mind—
And now we sacrifice our love upon
The altar of the idol we have made.

### XLIX.

To know what you have said of me I'd give
    The best years of what little life I own,
And all in me that will for ever live
    To know what you have thought of me alone.

## L.

O WAVES gigantic that roaring break
And hurl yourselves on a desert strand,
Wrapt in a sheet of the foam you make
    Drag me below with you, bear me on high.

O hurricane, driving with whips of wind
The faded leaves from the forest grand,
Dragged along by the whirlwind blind
    Goad me to go with you, prone as I lie.

O clouds of the tempest, by light'ning kiss'd,
Your edges shot with the fire of its love,
Whirled along in the sombre mist
    Bear me away with you, bear me above.

O bear me away with you, bear me away
Where frenzied with vertigo mad I may slay
My reason and memory, for I fear
    To be left all alone with my sorrow here.

## LI.

THOSE sombre-hued swallows again will stray
  To thy balcony, love, there to build them a nest;
  As they fly to and fro in a vague unrest
They will call to thee, call to thee at their play.

But those who lingered our names to learn,
  To drink in the sweetness of all they saw—
  My bliss and thy beauty without a flaw—
They will never return, they will never return.

The thick honeysuckles that clustering bind
  Thy garden-walls will return to their bride,
  And more lovely than ever at eventide
Will open their hearts to the wandering wind.

But those that are laden with dew-drops that yearn
  For the earth, and tremble and fall in our sight,
  Like tears of the day for the death of the night,
They will never return, they will never return.

Love's passionate words again will make
  In thy listening ears their luscious sound,
  And thy heart from the depths of its slumber profound
Perchance will awake, perchance will awake.

But the love of the worshipper for the Divine,
  As he kneels toward the altar and gazes above,
  Such love as I've given, believe me, my love,
Will never be thine again, never be thine.


## LII.

WHEN from out our happy past
  The flying hours we call,
A tear-drop glitters upon your eye
  And trembles, just ready to fall.

And at length it falls at the thought that we both
  Shall return to lament alway,
As the day that is for the day that was
  And the day that's to come for to-day.

### LIII.

To-DAY like yesterday and like to-day
　To-morrow—e'er the same !
Horizon limitless, and sky of gray,
　Life, motion without aim.

The heart with slow and rhythmic movement creeps
　A mere machine, while prone
And crowned with poppies in the corner sleeps
　The mind, dead as a stone !

The soul that paints the paradise of yore,
　But seeks it with despair ;
Toil without object, waves that roll and roar,
　Not knowing why or where !

A voice like the cuckoo that ceaseless calls
　In drowsy minor key ;
A water-drop monotonous that falls
　And falls incessantly !

So drearily they creep and creep along,
　The heavy-footed days,
To-day like yesterday—the self-same song,
　A joyless, painless phrase.

Ah, sometimes sighing I recall the pain
  My sorrows used to give—
Bitter is grief, yet happiness is vain ;
  To suffer is to live.

### LIV.

It is not strange this framework here
Of skin and bones at last has grown
So loath to bear my madcap brain ;
'Tis true I am not old and sere,
But from the cup of life I own
I drink so eagerly the pain,
A century of life, I'd say,
I've fused and poured into each day.

And so to-day were I to die,
That I have lived I'd not deny ;
Without the house seems new and gay,
Within live ruin and decay.

Decay sits there, alas !   His wizened face
My sorrow ever mirrors to me now :
For there's a grief that passing stamps its trace
Deep in the heart, if not upon the brow.

### LV.

You wish there were no dregs in this sweet wine,
      No bitterness and gall?
Well, sip it, merely touch it to your lips,
      Then leave it,—that is all.

One sweet remembrance of this love you wish
      To keep?   To-day engross
Ourselves with love ; to-morrow let us say,
      Adios !

### LVI.

The object of your sighs
      I surmise ;
Your languishing ennui
      I can see,
For you cover its sweet cause
      With a gauze !
Child, you laugh ?   Well, by-and-by
      You'll know why !
You suspect ?   Perchance 'tis so,
      But I know !

Yes, I know the joy that gleams
    Through your dreams,
Lighting up the sights you see
    With its glee ;
And your forehead is a book
    To my look.
Child, you laugh?  Well, by-and-by
    You'll know why !
You suspect ?  Perchance 'tis so,
    But I know !


Smiles and tears play hide-and-seek
    On your cheek.
I know why,—ah ! do not start !
    Your sweet heart
Is a very easy scroll
    To unroll !
Child, you laugh?  Well, by-and-by
    You'll know why !
You know naught, and all you feel
    You reveal ;
I have felt—'twas long ago—
    And I know !

## LVII.

My life is but a waste; each flow'r
I touch withers within an hour;
For on my path some one must creep
Sowing evils that I reap.

## LVIII.

When the sleepless fever comes
And the hours creep slowly by,
On the border of my bed
Who will sit beside me?

When my thin and trembling hand
I stretch out—about to die—
Longing for a friendly hand,
Who will grasp it tightly?

When my eyes are glazed by death—
Eyes that ne'er again will see—
Should my eyelids open stay,
Who will close them kindly?

When they sound the funeral bell
(If a knell be tolled for me),
Hearing it, a gentle prayer
    Who will murmur softly?

When my body lies at rest
In the bosom of the earth,
O'er the soon-forgotten grave
    Who will come to mourn me?

When the sun returns to shine
On the morrow, in their mirth
That I passed once through this world
    Who will e'er remember?

## LIX.

TREMBLING comes the dawn at first, and scarcely dares to
    pierce the night,
Then it sparkles, grows, expanding in a burning burst of
    light.
Light is joy, the fearful shadows are the griefs that on me
    weigh.
Ah! upon my spirit's darkness when will come the dawn
    of day?

### LX.

FROM a dark corner of the mind
　　Past memories
Fly to beset me, like a swarm
　　Of angry bees.

Attacked, surrounded, 'tis in vain
　　I try to fling.
Them off ; each thrusts into my soul
　　Its poisoned sting.

### LXI.

THE miser guards his hoard ; so guarded I
　　My grief ; I wished to prove
That there existed something infinite
To her who swore to me eternal love.

To-day I call on it in vain ; I hear
　　Time, who destroyed it, say,
You are not able e'en to suffer pain
Eternally, poor miserable clay !

## LXII.

NIGHT came, but no shelter I found,
  I'd but tears to quench my thirst.
  My hot eyes were ready to burst,
And, fainting, I fell to the ground.


In a desert I seemed to be ;
  Though I heard the hoarse multitude's drone,
  I was orphan and poor and alone,—
The earth was a desert to me !


## LXIII.

WHENCE come I? Seek the darkest, roughest way.
  Upon the stones the tracks of bleeding feet
  And on the thorns a heart transfix'd will meet
Your eyes ;—they'll tell you where my cradle lay.


Where go I? Cross a waste of endless gloom—
  Vale of eternal fogs and snows. Where lone
  And melancholy stands a nameless stone,
Where dwells oblivion, there will be my tomb.

## LXIV.

How beautiful it is to see the day
Arising, crowned with fire, the waves that play,—
      Each one a gleaming sprite,—
The air enkindled by the kiss of light !

Late in an autumn day, when rain-drops cloy
The flowers, how sweet and beautiful the joy
      To have your being fed
Upon their perfume till it's surfeited !

Upon a winter's eve, when silently
The snow-flakes fall, how beautiful to see
      The reddish tongues of great
And massive flames timidly palpitate !

When softly drowsiness begins to creep
Upon you, oh, how sweet it is to sleep !
      How good to drink and stuff
Ourselves ! A pity 'tis, 'tis not enough !

## LXV.

I KNOW not what I dreamed
Last night ; it must have pained
Me much, that baleful, melancholy dream,
For when I woke the anguish still remained.

On sitting up I found
The pillow wet with tears,
And for the first time felt, on seeing it,
My soul swell with a joy that cuts and sears.

Sorrow's pale offspring such
A poignant dream must be,
But in my grief I have one joy—to know
That tears at least have not deserted me !

## LXVI.

AT the flash of a light we are born ; we are dead
Ere its splendour refulgent is sped,—
Life is so short !
For glory and love that we ardently court
Are but shades of a dream that floats by ;—
To awake is to die !

### LXVII.

How often in the dead of night close by
    Those old moss·covered walls
That shelter her, I have heard the tinkling bell
    That to the Matins calls !

How often has the silver moon outlined
    My sombre shadow, near
That of the cypress-tree, which o'er the walls
    Leans from the churchyard drear !

When night has wrapped her robe around the church
    How often have I seen
Upon the windows of its chiselled vault
    The dim lamp's trembling sheen !

Although through all the angles of the tow'r
    The wind would moan, I'd hear,
Swelling above the voices of the choir,
    Her voice vibrant and clear.

If on a winter's night a coward dared
    Through the deserted place
To pass, on seeing me he'd cross himself
    And hurry on apace.

No doubt next day some crone would mutter to
    Herself, " It must have been
The ghost accurst of some old sacristan
    Who died, unshriven, in sin."

The corners of the porch before the church
    I knew e'en in the dark ;
Perhaps the nettles that grew there on which
    I stamped still keep the mark.

The frightened owls that with their flaming eyes
    Blinked at me, in the end,
When time had calmed their fears, began to look
    Upon me as a friend.

Beside me without fear the reptiles used
    To crawl and creep ; at last
I even saw the very granite Saints
    Salute me as I passed.

### LXVIII.

I DID not sleep, but in that region dim
I wandered, where all objects strangely limn
Themselves—bridges mysterious that span
      The sleep and wake of man.

Wild thoughts, that in a silent circle sped
And whirled and danced delirious through my head,
Little by little slowed their steps, to rhyme
     Them to a gentler time.

My eyelids veiled the reflex of the light
That through the eye enters the soul, but bright
And strong that other light shot with its beams
     The inner world of dreams.

'Twas then that softly sounded in my ear
A murmur vague, confused, like that we hear
In church, when to the roof the echo bears
     The " Amen " to the prayers.

I smelt the incense and humidity,
The candles just gone out ; it seemed to me
That from afar a sad, thin voice there came
     That called me by my name.

    *    *    *    *    *    *    *    *

Night came, and like a stone I sank to rest,
Clasped in Oblivion's arms, upon her breast ;
I slept and slept, and on awaking said,
     " Some one I loved is dead ! "

## LXIX.

### First Voice.

Let the waves with music thrill,
Sweetness in a rose recline,
Give her silver veil to Night
And to Day his gold and light ;
I have something better still—
　　Love is mine !　Love is mine !


### Second Voice.

Wave that kisses envy's feet,
Breeze of praise and cloud of flame,
Isle of visions, where of rest
Eager spirits go in quest,
Drunkenness ecstatic, sweet,—
　　Such is Fame !　Such is Fame !


### Third Voice.

Torch that shines from zone to zone,
Shade which vanity would flee ;
Aught else in the world's a lie,—
Glory, love and gold,—what I
Worship, that is truth alone—
　　Liberty !　Liberty !

While singing so the same eternal song
    The boatmen passed along,
And round the dipping oars the white spray spun,
    Struck by the sun.

" Do you embark ? " they shouted ; " Ah ! no more,"
    I said; " See on the shore
The token of my voyage—the clothes that lie
    Stretched out to dry ! "

## LXX.

THEY gently closed the eyes
Which open had remained,
And with a snowy cloth
    They hid her face ;
Then from the dreary room,
Some crying bitterly,
Others in silence stern,
    They all went forth.


The light that in a jar
Burned on the ground threw sharp
The shadow of the bed
    Against the wall ;
On it at intervals
You'd see the corpse's form,
Rigid and thin, weirdly
    Outline itself.


The day awaking smiled,
And with its thousand dins
The many-throated town
    Also awoke.

Before the contrast there
Of light and darkness and
Of life and mysteries
    I thought, " O God,
How lonely do we leave the dead ! "


Upon their shoulders broad
From out the house they bore
The coffin to the church
    And laid it down
Within the chapel.   There
With yellow candles and
With black cloths circled they
    Her pale remains.


Slowly they tolled the bell.
Hearing the knell, a gaunt
And shrivelled crone finished
    Her muttered prayers ;
Hobbling she crossed the nave,
The portals creaked and groaned,
Leaving the sacred place
    Deserted, still.

An old cracked clock with slow
And measured pendulum,
Some sputtering candles—these
    Alone were heard.
'Twas all so terrible,
So dreary and so dark,
So still and petrified,
    I thought, " O God,
How lonely do we leave the dead ! "


The high bell's iron tongue,
Slow swinging to and fro,
With pitiful lament
    Bade her farewell.
With mourning on their dress,
The relatives and friends
That formed the long cortege
    Passed by in file.


At one end of her last
And sacred resting-place
The pickaxe cut a niche,
    Narrow and dark.

Therein they laid her down,
And walled it afterwards.
The mourners with bowed heads
Then said farewell.


Pickaxe on shoulder borne,
The grave-digger walked on
Humming an air, and soon
Was lost to sight.
Night came with her black wand
And ushered silence in ;
Among the shadows lost
I thought, "O God,
How lonely do we leave the dead ! "


In the long dreary nights
Of icy winter, when
The tyrant storm-wind makes
The timbers groan,
And the mad rain beats fierce
Against the windows, all
Alone I sit and think
Of that poor girl.

There ceaseless falls the rain
With its eternal sound,
And battles with loud blasts
    Of wintry wind.
Stretched in the hollow there
Of that damp, dripping wall
Perchance her very bones
    Freeze with the cold !

Returns the dust to dust ?
To Heaven flies the soul ?
Is all vile matter then
    Ashes and rot ?
I do not know, but yet
There's something I cannot
Explain that makes us loath
    And sad to leave
The dead so mournful and so lone !

### LXXI.

THEIR robes ungirded, with halos wreathed,
Two angels watched with their swords unsheathed,
  On the golden lintel o'er the door.

I approached the strong gratings defending e'er
The entrance, and through them I saw her there,
  Indistinct and white in a misty light.

She appeared like the phantoms that flit through a dream,
Like the rays of light that doubtfully gleam
  And timidly swim through the shadows dim.

I trembled and shook and felt with a thrill
That my spirit was lured against its will,
  Toward the mystery drawn, as by gulfs that yawn—

But the angels that stood there seemed to say,
"None that is mortal may ever stray
  The threshold o'er of the golden door."

## LXXII.

Is it true that from its prison
  In swift flight our spirit slips,
When sweet sleep our drooping eyelids
  With his rosy fingers tips ?

Is it true our soul at midnight,
  Borne on wings of breezes fleet,
Mounts into the spaceless ether,
  There with other souls to meet?

Is it true our naked spirit,
  With no earthly fetters fraught,
For a while goes freely roaming
  In the silent world of thought ?

That it keeps the stain of passions—
  Joys that bloom and woes that blight—
Like the track left in the heavens
  By a meteor in flight?

Is this world of dreams without us,
  Or within us does it flow ?
I know only this—that many
  Whom I never saw I know !

## LXXIII.

IN the imposing nave
Of the Byzantine fane,
In that uncertain light which trembled through
The pictured glass, I saw the Gothic tomb.

Her hands upon her breast
And in her hands a book,
A woman beautiful reposed above
An urn—a piece of wondrous workmanship.

Her body sinking down
With its sweet weight had shaped
The bed of granite to its curves, as if
Of feathers and soft satin it were made.

The brilliancy divine
Of a last smile the face
Still kept, as keeps the sky at eventide
The dying glance of the departing sun—

Two angels seated on
The stony pillow's edge,
Ever kept watch, their fingers to their lips,
Imposing silence in the sacred place—

Death had so sweetly smiled
That she appeared to sleep
Within the shadow of the massive arch,
And to behold in dreams a paradise.

As one with footsteps soft
Draws near the cradle where
A sleeping baby lies, so gently I
Approached the sombre angle of the nave,

And for a while I gazed
Upon her, and that mild
Effulgence, that stone bed which offered there
Next to the wall another empty place

Inspired into my soul
Thirst for the infinite,
A longing for that life beyond, in which
The centuries are but a flash of time.

※　※　※　※　※　※　※　※

Tired of the endless strife,
Struggling in which I live,
Sometimes with envy I remember that
Dark, hidden corner and that woman fair,

Lying there mute and pale,
And say : "Ah me ! what love
As peaceful as the love of death !  What sleep
As tranquil as the sleep within the tomb ! "